Cataclysm

Vera Clover

Contents

Into The World

D ark.

Dark.

Dark.

Dark.

Screaming.

Speaking.

"One more push!"

English language. Female. Approximately 45 years.

Light.

Bright light.

Closer.

Closer.

Blinding light.

"It's a girl!"

Warm. Human body. 99 degrees even. Slightly wet. Salty smell.

Something touches my face. I open my eyes, peering at the female in front of me.

Oblong face. Brown hair. Brown eyes. Sharp nose. Soft eyes. Thin lips. Small ears. 27 years?

Her eyes widen and her body shakes.

"What's wrong with her eyes?"

My eyes? I blink. Nothing. My sight is just fine considering the light from a single light bulb hanging above me. Another female appears in my line of sight.

"Oh my. I'll take care of that right now."

She disappears and the female holding me pays close attention to every object and sight besides me.

A sharp object enters my body through the flesh on my upper arm. I feel the drugs maneuver through my veins. The effect hits milliseconds later. My eyelids become oddly heavy. I am barely capable of keeping them open. Soon enough, they close and refuse to open. All my senses shut down, leaving me to float in my thoughts.

Abandoned

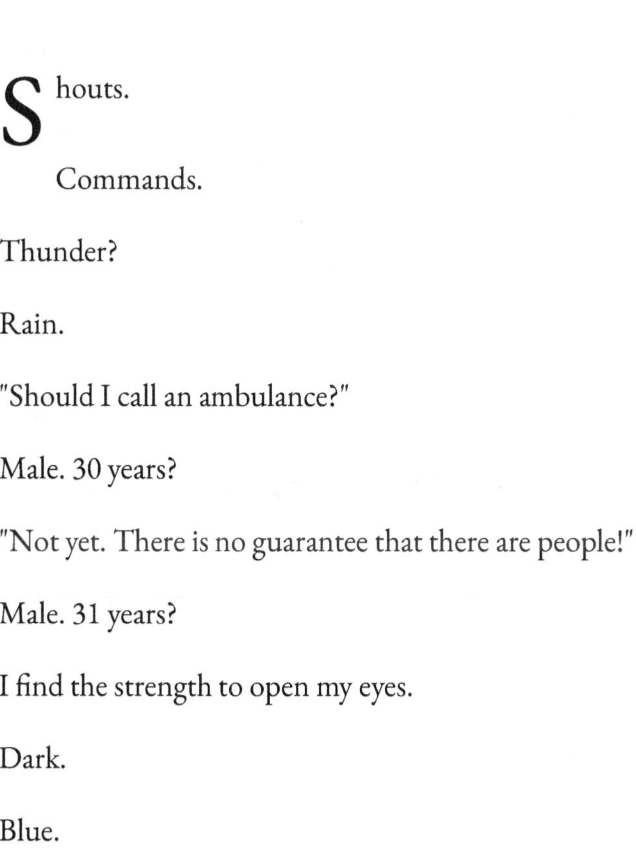

S houts.

Commands.

Thunder?

Rain.

"Should I call an ambulance?"

Male. 30 years?

"Not yet. There is no guarantee that there are people!"

Male. 31 years?

I find the strength to open my eyes.

Dark.

Blue.

Gray.

Black.

The colors of the night surround me.

Once lone beam of yellow light hits a reflective object. It shines in my eyes. I jerk my head, getting the harsh light out of my eyes.

"Something moved!"

Footsteps.

Cracking.

Rustling.

Bright light returns to my body. A body covered in a fabric of some kind.

"There's a baby!"

"I'll call the ambulance!"

"No! They'll take too long to get here! We have to take it to the hospital!"

It? I am referred to as It now?

Round face. Black hair. Blue eyes. Thin lips. Medium ears. Straight nose.

This man grabs the small body I inhabit, carrying me into the darkness. My eyelids get the heavy feeling again, drawing me right back to my pool of thoughts.

Small Human Fetus

S irens.

Louder.

Louder.

Louder.

Crying.

Strange smell.

Bleach?

Disinfectant?

"I need a nurse."

Male carrying me rushes me over to a female. 29 years?

"Oh my gosh, sir! A baby! Follow me."

Baby? Small human fetus. Baby. Yes. I am a baby.

"Set the baby here."

He does as she says and the fabric covering me is removed. A device on the wall is grabbed by female and she speaks into it.

"I need diapers and a pediatrician down in the emergency room."

Device is placed back on wall. New female enters room.

Cold.

Something cold touches my bare skin on my torso. I squirm in discomfort. Cold is taken off my chest.

"She is so cute. What's her name?"

37 years.

Now I see the other male.

Round face. Blonde hair. Blue eyes. Full lips. Medium ears. Wavy nose.

Black hair responds.

"Cataclysm."

The new female nods.

"Gorgeous and unique. How did you come up with it?"

New female pokes at my flesh with tools, shines light in my face. I open my mouth to protest but all that comes out is a cry of distress. I close my mouth, shocked.

No form of communication.

No verbal communication.

"I know, baby girl. You're okay."

She finally gets to my eyes, pushing the eyelids back to open them wide.

She finally gets a glimpse of the thing that shocked the other females.

"Her eyes! What a beautiful color, but what on earth is wrong with them?"

The black and blonde hair males look at my eyes and I scream in protest.

"Just something about pigment. Nothing serious."

"I've never seen a baby with such dark, crimson eyes before."

A Fitting Name

D^{ark.}

Crimson

Red

Eyes

Is that what scared away the two woman I saw first? My eyes? A deep red color frightened humans away?

"Her eyes were a perfect surprise we got the day she was born and we got to take her home."

"She's only a couple hours old. Why is she here?"

Hours? I have been alive for hours? The human body's need for hibernation must be taking large chunks of time out of my life.

"She was hot. I thought she might have a fever."

"It's normal for new parents to overreact to certain things. It's good to be aware of your child. Let me check everything once again and I'll send you home with her."

"Thank you."

The female, 37 year old Dr. Walsh, checks me over again. Black and blonde hair look exchange looks and words. I try to understand but the female is in my way. She pokes me and examines me before delivering words out of plump lips.

"She's perfectly healthy."

My mouth opens and the doctor smiles.

"And she's clearly tired. A newborn should be getting 16 or 17 hours of sleep a day."

"Thank you for the advice."

Something called a diaper is then removed from my body and a new one is put back on.

"Let her rest when she gets home."

"Okay. Thanks."

The male with black hair picks me up again.

"Come on, Cataclysm."

Cataclysm. My new name. I have a name.

Not It

Not Girl

Not baby.

Cataclysm.

A real name.

These thoughts make my eyes heavy again.

Starving

S trange.

Powder.

Soap.

Vanilla?

"What are people going to think? We haven't even talked about children!"

"We are two adults, Zach. We can say it was a spur-of-the-moment decision."

"That's not the point! We just spent almost $1,000 on baby supplies! A crib, diapers, wipes, formula, bottles, baby this, baby that..."

"If you really don't want her, we can always drop her off somewhere safe. A fire station or something. Her parents must be out there somewhere."

"No. We took her on now. And her name. Cataclysm? Where did you get that name from?"

"Describing how she came into our lives. A horrible thunder storm. A violent natural disaster brought us a good thing."

"What about a middle name?"

"Who said we have to pick one out?"

"She needs one."

My eyes open. Dim light from a corner.

Where?

Something is blocking my view. I'm in some sort of baby prison.

My need for food makes my stomach rumble. I open my mouth to communicate the word 'food' but all that comes out is a scream. That is going to get annoying fast. Soon enough, the black hair man comes into the room.

"There, there, baby girl. What do you need? Fresh diaper? Bottle?"

I screech at the word bottle, doing my best to 'say' yes.

"I got her, babe. Let me learn how to care for her"

"Okay. I'll make the bottle for her."

Bottle? If this so called 'bottle' doesn't have a steak in it, there's going to be some issues.

Blonde hair carries me downstairs to a room with gray cabinets. As I look around more, I realize what it is.

A black and white themed kitchen with stainless steel appliances.

Isn't that great? At hours old, I can think up difficult terms yet can't speak.

Oh the language barrier.

Beep.

I jump at the noise and my human body starts to cry.

Why am I crying at such a simple noise?

Why did it scare me?

Blonde man starts rocking me gently, shushing me.

"It's okay. It was just the microwave."

Mi-cro-wave.

Maybe being a small human fetus will aid me after all. New vocabulary words.

Something warm is shoved into my face. Liquid from this drips into my mouth. It actually doesn't taste bad. I wrap my lips around the object.

First Experience Of A Bottle

A drip here.

A drip there.

Nothing major.

Nothing satisfying.

I move my tongue against the tip angrily and the liquid starts to flow out.

The taste is unexplainably good.

When air starts entering my mouth instead of liquid, I realize I possess the need to empty my small bladder. How do I communicate this need to them?

"She might need her diaper changed in a bit. That was a lot of formula for her. She probably peed it all out!"

"I'll burp her first."

Burp me?

I am shifted until my head rests gently on the blond man's shoulder. Large living space.

Couch.

Chair.

Strange object with flashy pictures on its surface.

Pink torture device?

He pats my back with his hand repeatedly.

This is never going to work.

Some of the liquid comes up in the back of my throat. I'm going to be sick. Don't pat me again fleshy male!

His hand connects with my back and I have no choice to let the liquid out of my mouth.

He either doesn't notice or doesn't care since he continues on with patting my back until I let a gas bubble escape.

Black hair man moves to block my view of the living space.

"Hand me the baby, Zach."

"I got her."

"You have spit-up all over your shirt."

"What?"

Black hair man takes me away from blonde.

Zach?

Blonde has a name too!

Zach.

"Go change. Morris and Jane are coming over soon."

Black hair rocks me in his arms. I stare up at his face.

"You invited our friends over when we have a newborn?"

My eyes turn to the direction of Zach.

"They already were coming over today, remember? Dinner?"

Back to black hair.

"Yeah. Okay. What do we do about this demonic creature?"

My eyes move between each as they speak.

"She's a baby. Not a demonic creature."

"It was only a joke, babe. Calm down."

"I know you really didn't want kids, but what are we going to do? Force her into a foster care system that is crumbling?"

"Babe, relax."

Black hair has name to. Unique name.

Babe.

Zach moves his face to Babe's. Their lips press together. Babe smiles and take a step back from Zach.

"No kissing while I'm holding the baby. Save it for later."

When two human males press lips together it is called kissing.

Interesting.

Babe

B abe takes me over to the pink torture device, setting me down. It's surprisingly comfy and soft against my skin. He takes my arms, putting them through some sort of strap with two buckles. Both Babe and Zach sit on the couch next to each other.

"Good idea. The baby bouncer is a perfect place for her to relax when we are busy."

"That's not why I put her in here, Zach. We need to discuss our future. We have a child now."

"We have had this baby for nine hours and you are already acting different."

"I'm sorry. It's just going to be an adjustment for us both."

"I know, but we are allowed to have fun."

"We have to set a plan if someone comes looking for her."

"Like?"

"Are we going to return her to her family?"

They both look in my direction. I smile and try to say, 'Hello', but it comes out another opening of my mouth.

"She's tired. We should put her in her crib."

"Cataclysm can sleep in the bouncer. It's okay."

Babe stares at me and I analyze his expression. He lost something.

Human ?

Animal?

Object?

His eyes show sadness and a glimmer of hope. A shrill sound bounces off the wall of the house. My human body gets the urge to leak water from its eyes again.

My mouth opens and I let out a frightened cry. Babe comes over and unstraps me. Once I'm in his arms, I stop crying.

Ba-dum

Ba-dum

Ba-dum

The sound is coming from his chest. A steady beat that makes my eyelids betray me once more, causing me to slip back into the dark abyss that is my thoughts.

New Humans

Happy sounds.

Laughter!

Human laughter.

Three males. One Female.

Zach and Babe.

Two new humans.

Both 36 years?

Laughter floats over to me again. I shriek back in response, no tears.

"Can I get her?"

"Yeah. Just be careful."

"I will. It'll be good practice for October."

Strange female comes into living space and looks at me.

"Hey, baby girl. No need to cry."

I'm not crying, human. I am begging to be part of the conversation.

Her stomach is big. I am taken into her arms and cradled. She walks me the room with the laughter. Zach and Babe sit with strange male at the table.

"Isn't she adorable, Morris?"

"Yes. She is. Storm rescue proved to be beneficial. Congrats."

"Leave them be, Morris."

"It's alright, Jane. Kellin and I already agreed that if her real parents come forward about their missing daughter, we will return her."

Kellin?

Who is this 'Kellin'?

Babe speaks.

"Exactly. We couldn't just leave her out there or let her be put into the system."

"I understand. She has beautiful eyes by the way."

Thank you female human who possesses the name of Jane!

"What did you say her name was again?"

"Cataclysm December Oakley."

"Such a pretty name. Where is her nursery?"

"Across from our room, why?"

"She needs a diaper change."

"That's the fourth diaper today!"

Four?

I was recharging. When did I need a diaper change?

My bladder does feel empty.

"I'll change her. You enjoy yourself."

Jane passes my body to Babe. He strolls me down to my

Nursery?

What is a nursery?

I learn that it is the room that contains the baby prison when he brings me in there. I am put onto a table of some sorts and the fabric covering the lower half of my body is removed slowly.

"Hey, baby girl. I'm Kellin. I'm one of your dads."

One?

How many am I supposed to have?

Two?

Three?

Four?

Wait! Babe is not black hair man's name? It's Kellin?

So he is Kellin!

He takes out a new diaper from nowhere before replacing the soggy one that is swaddling my bottom.

"Let's go take you back out to the party."

Eternity

"I can't keep her, Hazel. She looks like the spawn of the devil!"

"But you can leave her at a fire station! Don't just leave her in the aftermath of a storm!"

"Too many questions!"

"I just don't want you to get in trouble, Eryn."

"Drive faster. I want to get rid of her ASAP. Maybe someone else will think of her as something other than the spawn of the devil."

My eyes open and I start crying. What was that?

Hazel?

Eryn?

Storm?

Devil spawn?

Eryn. The woman who held me in her arms. Oblong face.

Hazel. The woman who put a needle and drugs into me.

Who are they?

Strangers?

A creak makes me wail louder, now completely frightened.

98.6 degree hands pick me up.

"It's alright, Cataclysm."

Bab- Kellin cradles me against his chest. No fabric between my little fist and him as I reach out. I am put on the same table as earlier, a fresh diaper to replace my old one.

I didn't even realize I had relieved myself!

I am buttoned back up. As a payment for his kindness, I lower the volume of my screams down to a whimper. He settles us into a chair and starts to move.

Forward.

Back.

Forward.

Back.

Very calming, but it makes me notice how hungry I am. I start to cry a little louder, hoping he gets my cue.

He does not.

Instead, he put me on his shoulder, patting my back gently.

I don't have the need to burp. I need to get nutrients into me.

To give him a better signal, I scream louder.

Footsteps.

Zach enters the room, hand rubbing his eye.

"Did you change her?"

"Yes."

"Rock her?"

"Yes."

"Feed her?"

"Not yet."

"I'll go make a bottle."

Liquid food! I silence myself, pleased that I am going to get what I want.

"I think I calmed her down."

No! Feed me!

I scream again in protest. Silly human, why don't you understand me?

"Never mind."

Food

After an eternity, Zach returns with my sustenance.

When the tip enters my mouth, I greedily suck out the, as the humans call it, formula. The warm mixture hits my stomach and starts to fill it. The sensation makes my eyelids grow heavy, but I want to finish this!

I struggle to keep my eyes open and alert. Zach puts his lips on Kellin's head.

"She loves you already, Kellin. You're a great father."

He just nods and smiles in response. I am unable to keep my eyes open any longer. I try to smile back at Kellin, but I am unsure if I did.

The dreaded need for relaxation hits me and all my senses go black.

Gay

V oices.

Kellin.

Zach.

Arguing?

"I can't just call up my mother. She banished me the minute she found out I'm gay!"

Gay?

Definition please?

"She'll forget all about the fact that you like men after she sees Cataclysm."

Gay: when one likes men.

"I hope you are telling the truth here, Zach."

"Trust me. She'll forgive you,"

Beep.

Beep. Beep. Beep.

Beep. Beep. Beep.

Beep. Beep. Beep.

Silence. Silence. Silence.

"Mom? Hey. It's Kellin."

Quiet yelling.

"I know you said to never contact you again but I need you to come to our house."

Louder yelling.

"Mom! Please. Just trust me! I have something to show you."

Barely audible yelling.

"Okay. See you in ten minutes."

Click.

"She's on her way over. She's not happy."

"When is that woman ever happy?"

"Never."

"Exactly. Stop stressing. How about I take your mind off of things for a bit?"

I don't hear any response.

Grandmother

The same shrill scream from yesterday, now identified as a doorbell, bounces off the walls. It startles me at first, but I don't cry. Kellin approaches the door, opening it.

"This better be good."

"Come in, Mom. There is someone I want you to meet."

Footsteps.

Kellin and a new female walk into my view.

Gray hair. Blue eyes. Small ears and nose. Thin lips.

Kellin gestures to the bouncer I am in. When the woman spots me, she stops dead in her tracks, covering her mouth.

"Oh gosh!"

"Mom, I would like you to meet the newest edition to our family, Cataclysm."

"She is so gosh-darn adorable!"

"Would you like to hold her?"

"Of course I want to hold my granddaughter."

Kellin picks me up in his arms as the woman sits on the couch. I am transferred into her arms.

"Hey, beautiful. I'm your grandma."

Bladder full!

Bladder full!

Mayday!

Mayday!

I start to fuss. I need a way to relieve myself.

Oh wait. Diaper.

I give it a try, emptying my small bladder into the diaper. It works, but ew. I am now sitting in my warm, fresh urine. Now I let out a cry. The woman, my grandma, pokes the front of my diaper.

"I think she needs a change. Where's her nursery?"

"I'll take her."

"Nonsense. If I'm going to be watching my granddaughter, I will need to know where her nursery is."

"Mom, it's across from the bedroom Zach and I share."

"I don't care where you and Zachary sleep nor do I care what you do behind closed doors. You have a child now and will clearly be more responsible."

She rises from the couch, walking to my nursery. What I've now learned to be a changing table is where she places me. I let her complete the routine I have now grown used too. Once I am all dressed again, my need for food appears in my stomach again.

"She'll probably need a bottle soon. You always did. Empty your bladder, refill it, fall asleep."

I like this human! She understands me!

"I'll make her bottle. Want to feed her?"

"Don't even have to ask."

Female Version Of A Father

"**W**here did the note come from?"

"I just told you. The doorbell rang, I set Cat down in her bouncer, opened the door, and found this taped to it."

"This makes no sense! I mean, what kind of sick joke is this? 'I hope you take good care of my baby. I followed you after you took her. Don't worry, I don't want her back. Just, please take good care of her. She was born at the stroke of midnight, turning into September 23rd, during the terrible thunderstorm'. What sicko writes this kind of stuff?"

"Ok. The doctor said she was only hours old when we brought her into the ER, right?"

"Yeah."

"So what if this is correct? Yesterday was the 23rd and we found her at four in the morning. Hours apart."

"How long was she alone? Why didn't her mom leave her at a fire station?"

"I have no idea. All we can do is put this note behind us and raise her."

"The only benefit to getting that letter is now we know her official birth-day."

"And we know that the mother won't be coming after us for custody."

Long exhale of air.

"True. I'm going to check on her. You making dinner tonight or am I?"

"I will. She's in her bouncer."

Mother? What is a mother?

Is that the female version of a father?

6 Months Old

✱ **6 Months Old***

"Kellin! Get in here!"

Something drops in the kitchen. Kellin runs in and gets down next to Zach.

"What's wrong?"

"Nothing. Watch this."

Zach places his hand on my back, guiding me up so that I am sitting. He moves his hand away from me and smiles.

"She's sitting up all on her own!"

Kellin smiles, pushing his lips to Zach's. He does not speak any words. They both look at me and I move my arms in frustration.

If I were able, I would tell them to stop looking at me.

And I would have Zach stop making me sit up.

"She's growing up too fast."

"If you think this is bad, wait until she starts dating!"

"Don't even make me think of that, Kellin. Our daughter is not going to date until she's 18."

Date?

A day of the month

or year

as specified by a number?

What?

"Relax. It was only a joke."

"Still. I'm just glad I got to see her sitting up again before I head off to work."

"Again?"

"I've been trying to coax her for the past few days."

"That honestly doesn't surprise me."

"I'm just happy she is normal. Now if you don't mind, I have to go complete my crappy 9-5."

"You work 9-3."

"Same difference!"

With one more show of affection, Zach walks out of the living room and I look at Kellin. I move my arms in excitement, wiggling my legs on the floor. I feel myself tipping over. I hit the floor and squeal. No tears, just a shocked squeal.

Kellin picks me back up, perching me on his hip.

"Let's get you something to eat, Cat."

Cat.

The shortened version of my name Kellin and Zach have started to call me after Jane gave them the idea.

Not as good as Cataclysm, but I guess I have to deal with it until I develop communication skills.

Marriage

"**W**ant a beer, Morris?"

"No thanks. I have to get home to my wife and kid in one piece."

"Suit yourself."

Kellin sits down with me on the floor, handing me one of my soft, squishy animals. For no reason other than the fact that nobody is going to stop me, I put it in my mouth.

Yuck.

It doesn't taste good.

Yet, I still keep it in my mouth, sucking on it.

"How is Jane adjusting to life as a mom?"

"Just as you can expect. She's doing fine. Dario has yet to sleep straight through a night."

"Cataclysm took forever to sleep through a night."

"That is just what I wanted to hear."

"Didn't read any parenting books?"

"No. Did you?"

"We rescued Cat, how could we have read any parenting books in advance?"

"Good point."

Morris picks at his hands and Kellin continues to interact with me.

"So are you and Zach ever going to get married?"

Kellin's reaction is pure shock.

"What made you think of this?"

"I was just thinking of benefits to being married when you have kids."

"We actually haven't discussed it."

"Not even since you took in a baby?"

"No. We've been busy with everything. Doctor appointments, work, and just family time in general has kept us pretty tied up recently."

Married? I have heard that word used before. To describe Jane and Morris! Married.

What does it mean though?

I take the soft animal out of my mouth, waving it around my head before it flies out of my hand and lands on the floor. Kellin grabs it, handing it back to me.

"Would you ever get married?"

"That's a hypothetical question, Morris."

"Not really. And I was just curious, no need to get defensive."

I didn't sense a defensive tone in Kellin's voice.

"How's Dario doing?"

"He's almost five months. He's doing everything a five month old is supposed to do."

"Would you ever have another?"

"Would you ever adopt another?"

"All depends."

"The same thing here."

A loud noise comes from Morris's leg. He pulls out a cellular device, putting it to his ear.

"Hey, sweetie."

Blah.

Blah.

Blah.

Blah.

Noise comes from the other end of the call.

"I'm on my way. Don't panic. I love you too. See you soon."

He hangs up, standing.

"That was Jane. Dario took an atomic dump and it's not pretty."

"So why is she calling you home?"

"I was the one who took care of it last time."

"Good luck with diaper duty, Morris."

"Thanks, some friend you are."

Just by the nature of their conversation, I can tell they are joking.

Baths

I open my mouth, taking the spoonful of delicious mush that Zach is feeding me. I clamp my mouth down and Zach slides out the spoon. I force my tongue to work against the roof of my mouth, pushing the taste stuff down my throat. I turn my head in his direction as Kellin enters the room.

"You just distracted the baby."

"Maybe I'll distract you instead."

He leans over and blocks my sight of Zach with his back. I know they are connecting lips just by the sound. Annoyed and hungry, I slap my hands on the tray in front of me. It manages to get their attention. Thankfully, Zach sticks another spoonful of that heavenly slop into my mouth. Disappointed by my interruption, Kellin whispers in Zach's ear as he continues to feed me.

Giggle.

Giggle.

Snort.

Stop taking his attention away from me eating!

I scream in protest and they both laugh.

"Call your mom and see if she is willing to take her to the park or something."

"At six in the afternoon, she's going to know exactly what's going on."

"Is she that smart?"

"Depends on the day."

"Just call her."

"Not now. We have to give Cataclysm a bath. Maybe later after she falls asleep? I can't wait to..."

The rest of his sentence is lost to me because he whispers it to Zach, making him blush furiously.

"All done!"

What?!

I look at the container, and sure enough, it's empty. My stomach feels full, so I can't complain. I'll pass it all later and then be hungry again.

"Bath time."

The cloth piece from around my neck is taken off and put on the kitchen counter as Kellin picks me up. I am carried to the upstairs bathroom that is located in Kellin and Zach's room.

Whoosh!

Water pours out of a bent tube near the end of the massive bathing station. From prior experiences here, I am aware that a smaller bathing station is sitting, ready for me, in the larger one.

I am taken out of every last piece of clothing and the air hits me. Kellin climbs into the bathing station while Zach bounces me on his knee. The water shuts off and I am handed over to Kellin. He lays me down in the net-like material, placing a soaked washcloth on my lower half before starting the process of putting slippery soap on my body.

Strange Noises

T hump

Thump

Thump

What is that sound? I look around my nursery as best I can. Nothing I can see.

Using the skills Zach practiced over and over again with me, I sit up, looking around again.

Thump

Thump

Who or what is making that noise? Doesn't matter, I'm going to get my revenge. For sure.

A loud noise from outside of my nursery startles me. I start crying out of frustration and freight. . The thumping stops. Something creaks. Kellin appears in the doorway, clicking on the light to reveal his hair sticking up in every direction. He rubs his hand over his face before approaching my crib, where I extend my small, fleshy arms. He picks me up and I start to whimper instead, my cries quieting.

"It's okay, baby girl."

Zach stands in the doorway.

"I told you not to wake the baby."

"That definitely wasn't me."

"Whatever you want to think, go ahead."

"She's your daughter too, why don't you hold her?"

Okay."

I am passed from Kellin to Zach. Kellin walks out of the room and I smile up at Zach proudly.

"Now you got me in trouble with your Daddy."

Daddy? Is that a new form of the word Dad?

I move my mouth, trying to form the word.

D-a-d.

"Are you going to behave yourself, or am I going to be in here again in a few minutes because you're crying?"

I give him my best puzzled expression and he laughs before placing me back in the crib. He leaves the room, clicking off the light.

Click.

Squeak.

Nothing. No other noise joins the silent night. Just the sound of Zach going to recharging his human batteries.

Babysitting

"Here is some food for her. I packed a variety and there's diapers and wipes in her bag."

"Relax, Kellin. I can handle her for a few hours."

"Are you sure? I know you have your hands full with Dario."

"Yes. My sister said she was coming for a visit. I'm expecting her any moment."

"Okay. Please, don't be afraid to call me you need anything."

"Just go to work, Kellin!"

He smiles and leaves. Jane, who has me perched on her hip, smiles.

"Hey, baby girl. Go easy on me today, okay? You can play with Dario."

She takes me into her living room where a small human fetus like me is laying on fabric. Earlier, Jane referred to it as a play mat. The little baby has dark hair and blue eyes.

5 months old?

A mix of Jane and Morris' features.

Round face, small nose, medium ears, plump lips.

He is, in a small human way, cute.

Jane puts me on a mat almost like his, where I sit peacefully. She reaches into the bag that Kellin packed for me, pulling out my favorite toy in the whole world. A soft, round object with colors all over it. I am drawn to the texture and put it straight into my mouth before offering it to the other baby.

"Let me get the Boppy."

Jane grabs a green thing and sets it near us before laying the baby in it. It props him up a bit so he is easier to see.

I once again push the colorful thing to him, but he doesn't grab it. Fed up, I take it back. A doorbell sounds in the other room.

"It's open!"

A door opens and shuts, a new woman entering the house.

"Jane?"

"In the living room!"

Oblong face. Brown hair. Brown eyes. Sharp nose. Soft eyes. Thin lips. Small ears.

Jane stands up, hugging the woman.

"It's good to see you, sis. It's been, what, almost two years?"

"Yeah! I can see I've missed a lot. I mean, you have two babies?"

"No. Cataclysm isn't mine. I'm watching her for a friend."

"Oh."

"Yeah. Dario is though. Come meet your nephew."

The new woman sits on the ground with Jane and I study her carefully. I think I've seen her before.

Where?

When?

She takes a quick glance at me, a shocked expression on her face.

"Are her eyes... red?"

"Yeah. Something about the pigment being off or something like that. They are beautiful though, aren't they?"

"Very."

Her answer is hesitant. Jane passes her the other human fetus, Dario.

"I'm going to get a drink, want anything Eryn?"

Eryn?

I've heard that name before. Now I am sure of it.

"So where have you been?"

"I've been hanging out with Hazel. You know, going to concerts, site seeing, standard road trip around the grand old United States of America."

Hazel.

Eryn.

My dream.

Or nightmare.

I stare at the new Eryn human in shock.

She is the one who delivered me.

She is the one Kellin called my 'mom'.

If only I developed vocal communication skills, I would have been able to ask the questions burning in my mind.

Why did she leave me?

What is so wrong with my eyes?

Why is she not taking me back?

Sadly, by the time Kellin came back to pick me up, I still had not developed any new skills and my questions left unanswered.

Why can't I just talk!?!

I burst into tears out of frustration.

"It's okay. We're almost home. Don't cry."

I'm not crying over this device of straps holding me into the seat! I'm not screaming about being in a weird moving thing! I'm frustrated!

This just makes me cry louder.

When I am finally removed from the seat, I realize that I need to take a break. I listen to the thumping in Kellin's body, struggling to keep my eyes open. The movement carrying us to the front door is what finally causes me to give in, succumbing to the need to replenish my energy.

Crazy

"I didn't even know Jane had a sister."

"Neither did I, until I meant her today. Her name is Eryn, and I'm telling you, Zach, she looks very similar to Cat."

She is the one who brought me into the world!

"You're probably just seeing things. I'm sure Jane would have been aware if her sister had a baby."

No! Listen to Kellin! He isn't crazy!

"But Cat was abandoned."

So?

"Explain a bulging stomach."

Jane hasn't seen Eryn in years! Please, confront Eryn!

"You're probably right. I think I'm just afraid her mother will actually come and get her one day."

She was terrified of me! She won't want me. Her eyes showed hatred when she held me! Well, she showed it by leaving me in the middle of the huge world.

"I would say let's legally adopt her, but it's a little too late. And I wouldn't even know if she has a birth certificate."

A what?

"Let's just drop the subject. I'm sorry I brought it up. Tell me about your day at work?"

I don't listen to the rest of the conversation.

Trying Applesauce

I open my mouth wide, taking a spoonful of what Zach and Kellin refer to as applesauce. It is very tasty in comparison to the other things they have tried to feed me.

Stuff with names like prune apple or pear zucchini corn.

Not tasty at all!

"Zach, can you hand me a moist paper towel?"

"Sure."

The sink is turned on and off before something soars through the air and lands in Kellin's hands, dripping water on me in the process. I squeal my displeasure at them and they laugh.

Kellin then proceeds to put the wet, cool paper towel to my face, wiping away any food that slipped out.

"All done!"

Babble is all that comes out when I try and thank him for the yummy food.

Language barrier.

Not very fun.

"Is Jane babysitting again tomorrow? I have work."

Kellin takes the bowl from my meal and places it in the sink.

"She said she would. Apparently Eryn is visiting her again and it makes it easier."

"I guess it would. I mean, I love Cataclysm and all but I wouldn't be able to juggle two of her!"

Hey!

I'm not that much of a trouble maker!

"From what I've read and heard, she actually is a mellow baby."

"But can you imagine if we weren't that lucky?"

Kellin thinks for a few seconds before giving a physical response I am more than delighted to not see. Just the sounds alone make me mentally cringe.

I grab at the spoon Kellin forgot to grab, throwing it. I hear it clatter to the ground and that breaks apart the happy couple.

"Scratch that. She is a trouble maker."

I smile back at Kellin as he picks up the spoon. I shove my fist into my mouth.

Someone grabs me out of the chair and picks me up to spin me around. I know immediately that it is a behavior only exhibited by Zach.

"She just ate, babe."

"So?"

"Don't come crying to me later when you have to wash your clothes and you smell like baby vomit."

To any readers new or old, thanks for all the support!

Just out of curiosity, who is your favorite character so far? Comment the answer!

Don't be shy, let me know your thoughts!

Cheating

I watch as Dario swings his arms angrily.

Don't worry, smaller human fetus.

I was in the same position, but look at me now!

The doorbell rings and Jane shouts to the person about the door being open. I expect the woman who gave birth to me but it is a man.

"Peter! What are you doing here?"

"I couldn't just wait until you have a free moment. You tell me the most life altering news and expect me not to come over?"

"I don't want Morris to know!"

"I just wanted to come over and do this..."

They lock lips.

This isn't right!

She has Morris!

They separate and he kneels in front of her, pulling up her shirt.

"How's my little baby?"

Baby?

Another baby?

She already has a tiny human!

"Ultrasound says everything is good. I just have to find a way to tell Morris."

"That you are filing for divorce?"

"I can't do that, Peter. I love him."

"So you are going to have and raise our child with him?"

"There's no other option."

"Just get a divorce."

"I think it's time for you to leave."

His face drops to reveal sadness.

"I'm sorry. Please let me stay. Just for a little while."

Jane crosses her arms, glaring at him.

"Go wait upstairs. My sister should be here any minute to watch the kids."

Peter puts his lips on Jane's cheek and his hand on a part that makes me wish I didn't have eyes.

Afraid Of Her Baby

E ryn walks through the door a few minutes after Peter is hidden away upstairs.

"Hey. I have to shower. Can you watch the babies?"

Her eyes flick to me for a brief second, making her hesitate on her answer.

"Yeah."

"Thanks. All of Cataclysm's stuff is in her bag and you know where Dario's nursery is."

Jane follows the path Peter did minutes before. Eryn walks over and sits closer to Dario, avoiding looking at me. He starts crying and she picks him up.

"Looks like you need a diaper change."

After grabbing a diaper, she returns. Off with the old, on with the new. He's happy again! She disposes of the disgusting item, washing her hands. When she, again, pays no attention to me, I start up my babble, bored.

I try to communicate how I want my toy and how I know she is my 'mom', but she doesn't even glance in my direction.

This makes me mad.

I scream, making her jump. Knowing I have at least a fraction of her attention, I start wailing. Her reaction answers my unasked question.

She flinches and takes a step towards me.

"Please don't cry."

To make her mad, I scream louder.

She reaches into my bag, pulling out one of my toys. She gives it to me, careful not to touch me.

I turn the scream-volume up again, from a five to a seven. I cry like this for a while, watching her through teary eyes as she squirms in her place.

"What do you want from me?!"

Jane comes running down the stairs in gray pants and a purple top. She picks me up and I resort to happily babbling instead.

"All she wants is love and attention, Eryn."

"Well I clearly can't give that to her!"

"What are you talking about? You are amazing with Dario!"

"She's different!"

"How?"

"She's the spawn of Satan!"

"She's a harmless child!"

"Look at her eyes!"

"So what?"

"They are red!"

"Calm down!"

Eryn drops and curls up. I hear a creak. Looking at the stairs, I see Peter trying to sneak out. Just to be a pain-in-the-butt, I start crying. It attracts the attention of the woman who gave me life, drawing a puzzled expression to her face.

"Don't tell Morris! Please."

"Don't make me touch her and we have a deal."

No! Make her touch me! I won't hurt her! Please show her that!

"Deal!"

I just had to put these chapters up! Comments on your reaction to the next chapter! Please!

Answer Yes

"**S**he's just not acting the same. She doesn't seem bubbly and excited like normal."

Yes, human. Good detection. I am sad.

"Maybe she's constipated."

I am not constipated.

Kellin's hand connects with Zach's arm.

"I'm being serious. Something is up."

Yes. My biological flesh and blood doesn't want me. That's right, humans! I have learned more about a mother and father.

It is strange how we humans are created.

Made in factory and deposited into the womb of the female who designed us by a stork.

Peculiar.

"Take her to the doctor or something."

My attention is directed back to the conversation unfolding in front of me.

"Can you please be supportive here?"

"I don't have any siblings or anything so I don't know what to do!"

"I guess I'll just let it go for a few days, maybe she's just under the weather."

My temperature is 98.8 with a slight change of .2 here or there. I have no aches or pains. I am perfectly healthy. It is the fact that I am unwanted by the woman who I developed inside of for months.

"Can you run a bath?"

"Looking to have some fun tonight?"

"For the baby."

"Maybe one for us later?"

Zach's arm is rewarded with another hand kiss from Kellin.

"Why do I keep getting slapped?"

"I read somewhere that babies are like sponges and she is probably absorbing and cataloging your bad behaviors for the future. How would you feel if you knew that..."

The rest of the sentence is lost as Kellin lowers his voice, bringing his lips to Zach's ear. Zach's face turns bright red and his sudden change in body language suggests that he is furious.

"If I ever find out something like that is occurring, I will skin the person alive."

"Good choice of words, Zach. After I just informed you of possible situations, you go and tell our daughter that you want to skin someone alive."

Zach crouches down next to me, smiling.

"If any boy or girl ever hurts you, physically or mentally, I will protect you by skinning them alive."

I release excited babbles, Zach laughs, and Kellin groans, picking me up in his arms with his back to Zach.

"You are a terrible influence."

"If I am such a terrible influence, say no to my question."

"What question?"

Kellin turns as he speaks. He stops and gasps at the sight before us. Zach is on one knee with a small, sleek, shiny object nestled in a black box of some sort.

"Kellin Daniel Oakley, will you make me the happiest man alive and marry me?"

So?!?!? Thoughts?!?!?!

Celebration

Kellin's eyes go wide as he slowly understands what Morris is saying.

"You knew he was going to propose to me?"

There is a hint of anger and betrayal in his tone.

"Did you really think I just brought up that question out of the blue?"

"Kinda?"

"Well, I was doing research for a friend."

"And you didn't feel the need to tell me?"

"That would have ruined the surprise!"

Zach leans over me, whispering into Kellin's ear.

"If the surprise was ruined, all our fun would have never happened."

Kellin rolls him eyes.

"I'm sure it would have happened anyway. If you didn't start it, I would have."

Kellin then proceeds to take a sip of, what the group identified as, champagne, all while Zach's mouth is open with a shocked expression.

The food surrounding me smells good, but I have no way to aid digestion of solid properly with my lack of teeth. Instead, I look at the remnants of my apple and bananas.

"Is it okay if I run out to meet a friend quick?"

All eyes land on Jane, who is engrossed in a small electronic device called a 'cell phone'. Skeptical looks dart between Morris, Zach, and Kellin.

They know something.

They are all hesitant to respond, but Morris finally speaks up.

"Sure."

The air is heavy with tension. From who or for what reason, I am unable to determine.

I know it may seem like so few, but 120+ reads?!?!

You guys are amazing! Thanks for sticking with me!

Revenge

The music is turned down and changed.

"I told you I don't like her listening to songs with foul language and references to violence. She should be listening to child's music."

"She listens to that when you are driving. Let me be her reckless role model. Please?"

Thanks to my baby mirror, I can see Kellin turn to mush with the gaze Zach gives to him.

Not literal mush!

He is still a solid, muscular, boney, fleshy human.

Zach moves his hand to Kellin's lap, where Kellin jumps in his seat and then proceeds to smack it away.

"I'm driving!"

"Can I be her rule breaking father?"

"I know I'm not going to get you to stop."

"But you love me."

"That, I can't deny."

"Are you going to scold me if I put music back on?"

"No pop."

"No promises."

To drown out the response, Zach turns the dial and the music pours into the space.

'Oh baby lights on but your mom's not home. I'm sick of laying down alone. Hey. With this fever!'

"Really?"

"At least it isn't the standard songs about straight couples!"

Kellin shakes his head, smiling. The music changes. Zach starts singing and touching Kellin. An annoyed but amused groan comes from Kellin.

'There's a lot of people in the crowd, but only you can dance with me. So put your hands on my body and swing that round for me.'

With the push of a button, the song is changed to something else. I take my eyes away from the mirror, not wanting to see what Zach is doing.

'Take my body make it yours. So get up, we're gonna light this room on fire, yeah you and I will burn it up tonight, so get up, the two of us are gonna fuel this fire. No way in hell we're slowing down tonight.'

"Do you really feel the need to do this to me right now?"

'We're in positions that most people only say they know. You got you hand right on the landmine, ready to blow.'

"Zach..."

"I would ask what, but it is obvious why you are saying my name like that. You've got a big problem."

"Because of you!"

"Isn't the first, won't be the last."

The vehicle stops and the music is turned off.

"Take in Cataclysm."

"Going to take care of business?"

"Shut up."

Kellin walks, (waddles?), into the house and Zach takes me and my baby trap inside. He sets it down before taking me out and putting me in this weird netted cage they call a play pen. Bright lights and noises capture my attention, begging me to interact with them. But I am laying down on a soft fabric since I have failed to develop the necessary muscles to stand and walk.

Voices travel from somewhere else in the quiet house, landing straight in my ears.

"Let me help you out, Kellin."

"No. Go watch the baby."

"She's in her playpen."

"Go."

"But I feel responsible."

"You are."

"Come on. It'll only take a second."

"No."

My stomach rumbles and I start to feel a familiar discomfort. I need to make a bowel movement, or as Kellin and Zach call it, a poop. I start to relieve the feeling but something goes wrong. It is much more than expected. It starts leaking out of the diaper. It has an upsetting odor and it feels wet and sticky.

I start screaming, utterly disgusted by the actions of my body.

"Go. Get. The. Baby."

"It'll only tak-"

"GO!"

Footsteps approach the netted prison.

"I think it's time for a diaper change. You stink."

You have no real idea what I have done, human.

He reaches down, hands going under my arms. He lifts me up slightly and with one peek at the mess, Zach makes a strange sound.

Like a burp, but it's not a burp.

"Kellin! If you're done, I could use your help here!"

More footsteps.

"What's going on?"

"I think Cataclysm is getting revenge for our little scene in the car."

He also proceeds to make the weird burp sound at the sight.

"Okay. Go run a bath and grab a fresh diaper and a different outfit. I'll grab a rag towel and take her up."

I might not be able to update tomorrow, so here is another chapter! Enjoy!

Anybody know the songs off the top of their head? No cheating!

I Love You

My eyelids get that familiar heavy feeling as Kellin rocks me in a special chair. I can tell he is ready to recharge, too. His eyes close and open slowly, his breaths evening out. Zach comes into the room, his fleshy chest on display.

"Let me take her. You go to sleep."

I am handed over as Kellin leaves the room to satisfy the human needs of sleep. The warmth from Zach's body makes my eyelids even heavier.

"I don't know if you can understand what I'm about to say or anything, but I just want to let you know that we love you very much. I hope you remember this moment as you grow older. No matter what, Kellin and I love you. I know I can speak for him when I say that we will always be proud to be your fathers. I found a song earlier that I think you will grow to love."

He clears his throat before letting words slip out, following a tune that is playing in his head.

"'Dear daughter. Hold your head up high. There's a world outside that's passing by. Dear daughter. Never lose yourself. Remember that you're like nobody else. Life throws you into the unknown. And you feel like you're right there all alone. These are words that every girl should have a chance to hear.'"

He is cut off by the sound of another voice.

"Alright, Mr. Sappy. She's asleep."

No! My eyes are just closed! Please, keep that up.

I feel myself being placed into the wooden prison. Footsteps fade down the hall. Zach whispers one last thing before exiting.

"I love you, Cataclysm."

I know, kind human.

I love you too.

Congratulations?

B ang!

Bang!

Bang!

The noise scares me, causing me to cry. Kellin grabs me as Zach goes to see what is happening. A door opens and Morris comes storming in with Dario. At the sight, I stop crying.

"What's going on? Where's Jane?"

"She's pregnant!"

Both Zach and Kellin respond at the same time.

"What?"

"Jane is pregnant!"

"Uh... congratulations?"

"It's not my baby she's having!"

Peter said it is his baby!

"Oh sh-"

"Yeah! Some dude named Peter. She's been seeing him for several years already."

"I don't want to make the situation worse, but is Dario your kid?"

As response to his name, Dario squirms around, starting to fuss.

"Yeah. She said that he's mine."

"So what are you going to do?"

"Divorce her. That's my only option."

Divorce?

"What about the kid?"

"I'm going to file for full custody."

"Good luck. She's a convincing person who is good at manipulation and mind games."

"Don't think I learned my lesson, Zachary?"

He spits out the name like it is a bad taste in his mouth.

Wait.

Zachary?

Is Zach a shortened version like Cat is for me?

"No need to go throwing around words like that, Morris."

Kellin steps in, standing between the men.

"How about we all cool off? Calm down, think things through?"

"If I wanted sympathy, I would have gone to my mother's house."

"Put away the rulers and focus on the situation."

Rulers?

There is nothing in their hands. Just Dario in Morris' arms. With a long exhale of air, Zach speaks.

"I'm sorry, man. As if cheating isn't screwed up enough, she has to do it while you have a six month old kid? That is not right."

Dario is passed into Kellin's arms as water leaks out of Morris' eyes.

"I just didn't see it coming."

Zach pats his back.

"I know. Let's go get a drink."

They leave my sight as Kellin leans down and sets us babies on the couch.

I want to know what is happening! Don't do this to me! Take me with you!

My thoughts go unheard.

Fighting For Custody

Morris stops talking on his cellular device, feeding Dario instead. Zach makes a noise to draw my attention to the spoon of food he has ready for me.

"Who was on the phone?"

Pears!

Sweet flavor.

"Jane's lawyer."

Jane. That mean person.

"What about?"

"He wants to schedule a meeting with me and my lawyer next week."

"To discuss?"

"Divorce and custody."

Custody. Morris has said that word a total of seventeen times over two days. All in reference to Dario.

"I'm sorry to hear that."

"She's not getting Dario. I won't let her win. She can have whatever else she wants. I want custody of the baby."

Eighteen.

"Don't worry. You are more than suitable to be a single-father."

"Thanks."

"So where are you moving with the little guy?"

"My mother is letting me stay over for a little while."

Judging by the tone in his voice, he isn't a big fan of his mother.

"Good luck. Let us know if you need anything."

"Will do. Thanks for helping me adjust."

"If anybody can clean up an atomic crap, it's Kellin and I. Cataclysm delivered a nasty one the other day."

They laugh at my expense. To get revenge, on the next mouthful, I don't swallow. Instead, I send it right back out at him. He is momentarily shocked but smiles at me.

Dario's Future Lies In The Hands Of...

T he door opens and footsteps come into the house. I try to turn but the chair I am in is blocking my sight.

"How did the meeting go?"

"She didn't even fight. She just said, 'Take him. He's your kid anyway'."

I can hear the sadness in his voice.

"Does she have visitation?"

"She didn't want it."

"I'm sorry, man. Want to drown your sorrows?"

He is offered a dark brown bottle from the cold box thing.

"Rephrase it to small victories, but no. I have a son to raise on my own now and need to stay sober."

"I thought you were staying with your mother for the time being."

"I am. Darla doesn't like the thought of having a grandchild who has an absentee mother."

"First name with her now?"

"She doesn't deserve the title of mother."

"From the stories I've heard from you, I can understand why."

I relieve myself from an urgent bathroom matter before looking at Zach with pleading eyes.

"Follow me. Cat needs a diaper change."

I am picked up from the chair into Zach's arms.

"How do you know?"

"She always makes the same face when she needs a diaper change. I like to think she is communicating with me."

"Saying?"

"'Please change my diaper, weird thing that talks to me and cares for me.'"

I look up at him with wide eyes. He isn't far off. More like: 'This is unsanitary, please change it so I am clean again'.

"So you speak baby now?"

I send my best glare to Morris but I am ignored.

"I'm one of her fathers. I've grown close with Cat. I feel like we share a special bond already."

"Cause you were abandoned by your mother too?"

What?

The hurt in Zach's eyes says 'yes'.

He doesn't show it in his voice.

"She was a coward and a drug addict who attempted to have a fun night and popped me out later that year."

My back is against the cushion of the changing table.

"Looks like we all have crappy mothers here."

Unbuttoned onesie.

"Kellin's mom was actually pretty cool growing up."

Diaper unstrapped.

"Yeah. Until she found out her son was attracted to guys."

Moist, cold cloth to my sensitive skin.

"That's when it all went south. But here he is, years later with me as a fiancé and Cataclysm here as his beautiful daughter."

Fresh diaper.

When my name slips past his lips, Zach bounces me lightly.

Buttoned back up.

"Speaking of Cat, what are you going to do when she starts talking?"

Into Zach's arms.

"I'm more focused on getting her to crawl more often."

"She's crawling? Since when?"

I give Morris my best smile.

"Last week. She doesn't make it too far, though. Just enough to make Kellin whip out the video camera."

"Proud father moment right there."

"You can say that again."

Hey!

Just letting the readers who have stuck with me all this time know that there will be a sequel! A short story version, maybe a few chapters, but there will be more to Cataclysm's story!

Milestones

K ellin throws a pillow to the floor.

"Have you seen my phone?"

Zach enters the room with a towel on his shoulder.

"No. Why don't you call it?"

"I think it's on silent."

"I'll call it."

Zach pulls out his own device, tapping something, then he puts it to his ear. No sound comes from Kellin's. I only know that because I can see it.

I know where your cellular device is located! It is under the couch! It fell out when you sat to play with me!

I do my best to point but Kellin ignores me. I start with some angry babble, hoping to get him to see my gestures.

'Dad! Look!'

Wait. Dad? Is that what I am going to call Kellin and Zach?

Dad.

Strange.

Foreign.

Meaningful.

"Dada!"

Kellin and Zach freeze.

So do I.

Kellin turns to me slowly, registering what I just did. Zach is staring, open-mouth, in my direction.

It takes me a moment to figure it out, too.

I just said 'Dada'.

I can finally speak English!

Even if it is a small fragment of the vast language, it's better than nothing!

"Did she just do what I think she did?"

"Speak?"

"Yes."

I try the word again. It rolls off my tongue with ease.

"Dada."

They both start smiling.

"She just spoke!"

"We have to get her to do it again on video!"

Zach points his phone in my direction.

"Say it again, Cataclysm."

I'm not a circus animal who will do anything on command, strange human.

The pleading look in Kellin's eyes is what makes me do it.

"Dada."

Cheers.

One kiss.

One hug.

Two kisses on my head.

"Now is a really good time to start watching your language and music choice. We don't want her next word to be something inappropriate."

"Maybe you don't want it to be, but you can't speak for me."

The comment is rewarded with Kellin's eye-daggers shot in Zach's direction.

I mean, a glare.

"I'm only kidding, babe. Relax."

Another kiss is passed between Kellin and Zach.

>

And So He Knows

I shove my fist into my mouth, letting the piece of food soften. Music plays from Kellin's phone. He answers it, giving it a confused look.

"What's up, Morris?"

Screaming.

Panicked yells.

"Slow down! What about Cat?"

Quieter this time.

"I knew it!"

His face reveals something I can't detect. Too many mixed emotions.

"She's coming after her?! I need a lawyer. She abandoned her!"

Anger rolls off him in waves.

"She thinks she can knock you down by threatening me and my family? She's got another thing coming."

I stick out my fist, demanding more of the food. One is taken from the bag and placed in my open palm. I repeat the process and ram it into my mouth eagerly.

"I have to talk to Zach. There is no way Jane is getting Cat. Even if she is her biological aunt."

Mimicking A Female

My grandmother finishes fastening my diaper as she speaks with Kellin.

"So how is court going?"

"I'm not sure. There is no way that Eryn is getting off with a slap on the wrist. Zach's testimony was a tear-jerker."

"She left her newborn for dead! She deserves to rot in jail."

I kick my legs in protest as she tries to put on my pants. I hate pants. Too constricting and hot.

"Jane is trying to play the card of the clueless aunt."

"The what?"

His voice goes higher as he speaks, trying to mimic a female.

"'I didn't know my sister was pregnant. If she didn't want the baby, I would have taken her. I want to make it up to the baby and take her into my custody now.'"

"That is a load of crap!"

"Some woman name of Hazel is supposed to take the stand tomorrow to testify against Eryn."

"How does she fit into the case?"

"She delivered Cat and is Eryn's best friend."

"Why is she turning against her best friend?"

"To avoid a prison sentence. She made a deal. She only has to serve out a one year sentence as long as she testifies."

"What was her original sentence going to be?"

"Four years for aiding Eryn's disposal of Cat."

"Oh my."

"But according to Jeffries, her testimony should drive the final nail into Eryn's coffin."

"I hope it does. That monster doesn't deserve to ever have interaction with Cataclysm again."

She rubs the tip of her nose against mine gently in a loving manner. I smile, turning my head away to look at Kellin.

"You better win custody of this child or I am never going to speak with you again."

"You're a homophobe, so you speaking to me or not isn't really going to hinder my future."

"Kellin Daniel! Don't use that language around my granddaughter!"

I am taken from Grandma rather forcefully.

"It's the truth, and she is my daughter. I can use whatever language I want to around her."

"That's it! I'm not going to stand here and listen to your nonsense! Find a new babysitter for tomorrow!"

She storms out of the room, clearly angry. Kellin kisses my forehead.

"Don't listen to her, Cataclysm. She'll be back tomorrow. She just needs time to cool off. For now, let's get you some dinner."

I clap joyfully at the thought of eating.

r

Setting The Date

K ellin is right.

The next day, she returns to watch me.

And the next.

And the next.

On the fifth day of her watching me, Zach comes home with a smile from ear-to-ear.

"Dada!"

He picks me up off the floor, squeezing me gently to him.

"I'm assuming something good happened?

"We won! Cataclysm is officially our daughter!"

"That was quick."

"The jury was back in an hour with a guilty verdict. Eryn is going to spend the next ten years of her life in prison."

"That's excellent to hear."

"Best part, nobody from Eryn's side of the family can take her away!"

Yay!

I clap, hoping it is the correct reaction to Zach's obvious joy. If it is even possible, his smile gets even wider.

"What about her dad?"

"A random guy when she was drunk. Doesn't remember."

There is obvious tension between the two of them.

Hate?

"Where's Kellin?"

Yeah! Where's other human?

"He went to help Morris do something."

"When is he going to be back?"

"Soon. I think it was only lowering the crib for Dario."

"Well I have to be heading out. It was...pleasant...interacting with you, Zachary."

The word 'pleasant' is forced from her lips, almost like she was in pain when she said it. Zach gives a curt nod, dismissing her.

Not even a minute after we watch her car pull out of the driveway, Kellin's pulls in.

He rushes up the front steps, flinging open the door.

"Where's my baby girl?"

"Dada!"

I am, again, squeezed gently. Something wet brushes against my face.

Kellin is crying.

"She's ours, Zach. After fighting it out in court for an endless two weeks, she's finally ours."

"Calm down, babe. I know you're excited, but you need to take a deep breath."

He does, but it doesn't stop a fresh round of tears.

"What I need is you to be my husband. We need to get married now. Please"

Shock. That's what Zach's reaction is.

"Woah. I want to have a real wedding."

"Let's plan it for next week!"

I squirm in discomfort, not liking the overwhelming amount of excitement coming from Kellin.

"I want to wait until Cataclysm is able to walk down the aisle with a little basket of flowers."

"Okay. But the minute she starts to walk, we're setting the date. Got it?"

They seal their happiness with a long kiss. Disturbed by this display, I start screaming my protest. In response, they both laugh.

OH MY GOSH GUYS!!! THIS STORY IS NOW #981 IN GENERAL FICTION!!!

THANK YOU SO MUCH FOR ALL THE VOTES, READS, AND COMMENTS!!

Determination

✱ **One Year Old***

I wrap my chubby fingers around one of Zach's big ones.

I move my legs, propelling me forward. Zach tries to slip his fingers out discreetly, but I notice. The second he lets go of my hand, I plant my butt on the floor.

"She'll learn to walk on her own time, Zach. Relax."

"The wedding is next week."

"So?"

Disappointment oozes off of the words as Zach speaks them.

"I just wish she would be able to walk down the aisle on her own."

Kellin leans over, pressing a soft his on Zach's head.

"Just give it time. You can't force her to do something she isn't ready to do."

But I want to do this walking thing! I am tired of humans having to transport me everywhere! Teach me the secret to walking!

Again, my fingers put Zach's in a tight grip. I move one foot in front of the other, making my way over to Kellin. It is only a distance of, maybe, a foot. Nothing I haven't already completed over and over again on numerous occasions.

"We can ask Kathleen to help her walk down."

Kathleen. Morris' new friend. They did something by the name of 'elope' not too long ago.

"They have Dario to worry about."

My small human friend! He walks on his own, but only a few steps before his butt kisses the floor. It is very funny to watch! I laugh every time!

"Then we can ask your mom. Isn't she coming?"

"Yeah. Maybe she'll do it."

No. Nobody is going to walk me down the aisle.

I am quite unsure of what that means, but it means a lot to Zach for me to do it on my own.

And I will.

160+ reads already?!

Thanks!

Please share with all your friends, my goal is to get 200+ reads by the end of 2017!

Thanks again for all the support!

Frustration

T omorrow is 'the big day'. Or that's what Kellin and Zach call it.

All they do is talk on the phone and look on this one thing called a computer.

They don't pay attention to me as much.

Trying to please Zach's dream, I have started to utilize this time to practice the action of walking. I can pull myself up. I can walk.

Only while holding onto something.

It is a very frustrating process that is painfully slow.

"Where's Cataclysm?"

"In the living room."

Not anymore!

"No she isn't."

I have mastered the art of crawling. I am now in the room that is referred to as a bathroom.

Why?

Because I wanted to.

No rhyme or reason.

Just because.

"Cat?"

I get back onto my hands and knees, crawling towards the sound of his voice. When I hear his footsteps approaching, I sit and patiently wait. His worried figure steps into my view.

"Dada!"

Relief floods his face.

"There you are, troublemaker!"

I am offended by his words.

"Let's get you back to the living room."

He scoops me up and I squirm, wanting to be independently mobile again.

"Found her."

"Where was she?"

"In the hall. This is why we need baby gates."

Baby gates?

"Fine. We can buy them later. For now, we have to get to the rehearsal dinner."

Here comes the grooms!

The wedding is getting closer!

Rehearsal Biting

"**A**t this point in the ceremony, your daughter will come down the aisle with the rings."

I grab onto Grandma's fingers, two objects on a necklace around my neck. She aids me to the front of the strange new building I've never seen or heard of.

"Then we will take the rings and..."

Blah.

Blah.

Blah.

Big words and terms are exchanged that fly right over my head. I'm not old enough, or wise enough to comprehend that just yet!

"...and then you kiss and are pronounced husband and...husband."

I look towards my grandmother as she speaks with one of the other ladies.

"I'm shocked that a church would allow such an unholy ceremony to be performed in their presence. Homosexuality is a sin."

Just by the way she says the sentence, I know she is insulting Kellin and Zach. She tries to pick me up but clamp my jaws around her hand.

Ew.

She pulls her hand away. I know my two bottom teeth are too small to cause damage, but at least I made a point.

"Looks like she doesn't like you."

"She's a sin too."

The words hurt. I thought she loved me.

I burst out in tears, grabbing the attention of my fathers. Zach grabs me, bouncing me gently.

"What did you do to her?"

"That little brat tried to bite me!"

"She's a year old, mother! Give her a break!"

"I'm not going to stand around here and be insulted, again."

She turns, grabbing her bag, before stomping off to the back of the church.

"Don't show up for the ceremony tomorrow or I'll call the cops!"

Gasps erupt through the church but Kellin clearly doesn't care. Zach whispers, too quiet for anyone else to hear.

Hoping it's a funny, or correct, response to the situation, I start clapping.

"It's about time."

Kellin turns to us, his anger fading.

"How's my baby girl? Let me see those teeth."

He pokes my lip and I open my mouth for him, showing off my teeth.

The Big Day

Kathleen stands next to me, Dario in the arms of one of her friends. When she hears the cue, she reaches for my fingers. I grab onto them, looking at Zach. Sadness fills his eyes. This makes me upset.

Time to put my practice to the test.

I let go of Kathleen's fingers, taking a tentative step forward. I keep my balance, and when I don't fall, I keep going. It takes a moment for everyone, including me, to realize what is going on.

I'm walking.

And everyone is shocked at the sight. Zach's eyes are filled with tears.

Of joy?

Sadness?

Pride?

Disappointment?

I push forward, one step at a time. When I finally make it to where Zach and Kellin are waiting, I am kissed on the forehead.

Both of them whisper in my ear.

"Good job, Cat."

"Thank you, beautiful."

I smile at their reactions.

They are proud of me! I did it! I walked for Zach!

Someone directs me over to the waiting seat. Kathleen picks me up, setting me on her lap. I can't stop smiling.

I watch intently as Kellin and Zach, both dressed in fancy black 'monkey suits', as they call them, exchange words. The man in the funny clothes from yesterday finally says the command everyone was waiting for.

"You may now kiss the groom."

A long, loving kiss starts with everybody watching. Uncomfortable with this public display, I screech. Zach and Kellin break apart, smiling and laughing.

They are finally married.

Whatever that is.

They are husband and husband.

Whatever that means.

And I am their daughter.

And I am proud.

Evolved!

D on't forget, Evolved comes out 10/31/17!

Please continue to share Cataclysm!

I thank each and everyone of you for reading the story.

A quick update for Evolved:

Word count is currently 10,000+

There are 25+ parts all typed and ready

There IS a cast list (currently looking for someone to portray Kellin)

@SciFiFantasyNerd made the cover

@MaryFahey helped answer all my questions and concerns related to the book

Thank you for the 300+ views!

I am unbelievably grateful for your continued support and I look forward to seeing you all again on October 31st!